Brand-New Bubbe

Sarah Aronson

Illustrated by Ariel Landy

ɯ̈ɯ Charlesbridge

When Mom married Michael, Jillian got a really nice stepdad.
She also got a brand-new grandmother.
"Please! Call me Bubbe," she said.

Jillian already had her Noni and her Gram.
Bubbe didn't get the hint.

She smothered Jillian with bright
red kissy-lips that took a long
time to wash off.

She made plans for holidays Jillian had never heard of. And she was always kvelling—or was it kvetching?—whatever that meant.

"Wait until you taste my matzo ball soup," Bubbe said.
"It's the best soup in the universe!"

Jillian couldn't believe her ears. There was nothing better than Noni's meatball soup— except maybe Gram's spicy gazpacho.

She had no choice. In the name of grandmas, it was time for a protest!

When Bubbe gave her a teddy,
Jillian ignored it.

When Bubbe wanted
to shoot hoops,
Jillian refused to play.

And when Bubbe made dinner with all Jillian's
favorites, Jillian said, "I'm not hungry," and
"No, thank you," and "Please, may I be excused?"

That night, Mom had had it up to here.
"Don't you think you're being tough on your brand-new
bubbe?" she asked.
"Technically, we're not related," Jillian said.

Mom disagreed. "Family is more than blood," she said.
"Give Bubbe a chance." (And she wasn't asking.)

The next time Bubbe came to visit, her hands were full.

Jillian harrumphed all the way
down the stairs so that everyone
would know this was not at all
her idea.

Bubbe didn't seem a bit bothered. "Ready to
make soup?" she asked.

After preparing the broth, Bubbe told Jillian to get her hands good and wet. "If you use a gentle touch, the matzo balls will turn out fluffy and soft. If you don't, they'll sink like stones," she said.

"Where'd you learn that?" Jillian asked.
"From my bubbes, of course," Bubbe said,
offering Jillian a spoonful of broth.

Jillian couldn't deny that the broth was yummy.
Or that Bubbe was not at all horrible.

But she couldn't stop thinking about going to
the theater with Noni, or bike riding with Gram.
She didn't want them to feel left out. Or, even
worse, replaced.

After a lot of stewing and simmering—and
another bowl of that matzo ball soup—she came
up with a very good, very simple, very tasty plan.

You are invited
to a SUPER soup
celebration
PS. Don't forget your
pots and pans
I

All three grandmas arrived at the same time.

Dad showed up next. With him was Mom's
grandma, the Great Mama-Nana.

At first Jillian worried she'd made
a terrible mistake.

But pretty soon, the kitchen smelled like a delicious trip around the world. Even better, all three grandmas had a lot in common. Much more than soup.

Like soup, family was made with love.
And there was always room for more.

Aprons on! Hands washed! Surfaces clean and clear. Let's get ready to make some soup.

Safety tips: These recipes include chopping and cooking. Young soup makers will need help or supervision while handling sharp knives and stirring over hot stoves. Pots full of soup are heavier than they look. Chairs can be wobbly. Be sure to clean up spills when they happen. Cooking as a family is a lot of fun—working in the kitchen together adds the not-so-secret ingredient: love!

Bubbe's World-Famous Matzo Ball Soup

The world's best matzo ball soup begins with the world's best chicken broth, which is easy to make, as long as you're patient. Waiting is always hard, but the longer the broth simmers, the better it will taste! Every bubbe I know has a secret ingredient to make her broth extra special. My secret ingredient is parsnips. It makes the broth a tiny bit sweet, which works perfectly with slightly salty matzo balls.

You can make the broth and the matzo balls at the same time. Both take about 3 hours. Or you can make the broth ahead of time and reheat it when your matzo balls are ready.

For the broth:

1 whole chicken (4–5 pounds)
1 onion, outer skin removed
3–4 peeled carrots

3 stalks celery
1–2 peeled parsnips
salt and pepper to taste

1. Add the entire chicken (make sure to take out the giblets!) and the onion, carrots, celery, and parsnips to 2 quarts of cold water.
2. Heat to a boil, then reduce to a simmer and cover. Even though it's tempting, don't watch the pot. Chicken broth needs time—at least 2–3 hours, but sometimes I let it simmer even longer.

3. When the chicken starts to fall off the bone, add salt and pepper, then taste. (Blow first! It's hot!) You can simmer some more if you'd like to deepen the chicken flavor. When you're happy with the flavor, strain the broth into a separate pot. Discard the strained ingredients except for the chicken and carrots.
4. Remove the chicken bones and skin and shred the remaining meat. Cut the carrots into chunks and return the shredded chicken and carrots to the pot of broth.
5. Put the broth in the refrigerator to cool.
6. When the broth is cool, skim the fat off the top. The broth is now ready to use!

For the matzo balls:

1 teaspoon baking powder
1 cup matzo meal
¼ teaspoon ground nutmeg
2 tablespoons finely chopped fresh parsley or dill
1 teaspoon salt, plus more for cooking
black pepper to taste

4 large eggs
¼ cup schmaltz (rendered chicken fat), coconut oil, or vegetable oil (kosher for Passover)
¼ cup chicken stock or vegetable stock (from the batch you just made!)

1. In one bowl, combine the dry ingredients including the herbs and spices.
2. In a second bowl, whisk the eggs, schmaltz, and stock.
3. Gently add the dry ingredients to the wet ones with a spoon. Do not over-stir!
4. Cover the bowl with plastic wrap and refrigerate until chilled, at least 3 hours. (If you want to, you can refrigerate it overnight.)
5. Fill a wide, deep pot with lightly salted water and bring to a boil.
6. With wet, gentle hands, take some of the matzo ball mix and mold it into the size and shape of a Ping-Pong ball. Use a light touch. Do not over-mold. Do not squeeze too tight. (If you do, your matzo balls will have the consistency of rocks!)
7. Gently drop the ball into the boiling water.
8. Repeat until all the mix is used.
9. Cover the pot and reduce the heat to a simmer. (My bubbe taught me never to peek, so I never have. I don't know what would happen if I did.) Cook matzo balls about 30–40 minutes.
10. To serve, heat up the chicken broth from the recipe above. Put one matzo ball in each bowl. Ladle hot broth over the top and EAT.

Noni's Not-Just-for-Weddings Italian Wedding Soup

I love this soup for two reasons: meatballs (delicious in broth) and escarole. Escarole is a leafy green vegetable that's a little bitter when raw, but it's absolutely delicious when you put it in soup. No one I know has ever left any escarole in a bowl of wedding soup.

For the meatballs:

¾ pound ground chicken

½ pound chicken sausage, casings removed (I have substituted ground pork or turkey thigh for the sausage, and that works, too.)

⅔ cup fresh white bread crumbs

2 teaspoons minced garlic (2 cloves or more)

3 tablespoons chopped fresh parsley

¼ cup freshly grated Pecorino Romano cheese

¼ cup freshly grated Parmesan cheese

3 tablespoons whole milk

1 extra-large egg, lightly beaten

1 teaspoon kosher salt

½ teaspoon freshly ground black pepper

1. Preheat the oven to 350 degrees.
2. Place all the ingredients in a bowl and combine gently with a fork.
3. With a teaspoon, shape mixture into 1-inch balls and place onto a sheet pan lined with parchment paper.
4. Bake for 30 minutes, until cooked through and lightly browned.

For the soup:

2 tablespoons good olive oil

1 cup minced yellow onion

1 cup quarter-inch-diced carrots (3 carrots)

¾ cup quarter-inch-diced celery (2 stalks)

10 cups homemade chicken stock (Use Bubbe's broth recipe.)

1 cup small dried pasta

¼ cup minced fresh dill

salt and pepper to taste

12 ounces escarole, washed and trimmed

freshly grated Parmesan cheese for serving

1. While the meatballs are cooking, heat the olive oil in a large, heavy-bottomed soup pot over medium heat.
2. Add the onion, carrots, and celery and sauté until softened, stirring occasionally.
3. Add the chicken stock and bring to a boil.
4. Lower the heat and add the pasta to the simmering broth. Cook until the pasta is tender.
5. Add the dill and meatballs to the soup and simmer for one minute.
6. Add salt and pepper to taste.
7. Stir in the fresh escarole and cook for one minute, or until it is just wilted.
8. Ladle into soup bowls and sprinkle each serving with freshly grated Parmesan cheese. A piece of garlic toast makes this a fantastic meal!

Gram's Easy-Peasy As-Spicy-As-You-Like-It Gazpacho

This is what I call summer! It's refreshing. It's healthy. It's spicy. And it's the easiest soup in the world to make. There's no cooking at all!

The ingredients:

1–2 English cucumbers, cut into chunks
1 red onion, skinned
1 red pepper
3 cloves of garlic (or more!), peeled
1 46-ounce bottle of tomato or
   vegetable juice
3 teaspoons sherry vinegar
   (or red wine vinegar)

2 teaspoons Worcestershire sauce
¼ cup olive oil
salt and pepper to taste
1 fresh hot pepper, seeded and diced
avocado slices, toasted croutons, and/or
   cilantro for garnish

Ready to cook without cooking?

1. Put the cucumber, onion, pepper, and garlic into a food processor or blender, and blend to your desired texture. (This gram likes her gazpacho slightly chunky, but smooth is great, too.) Save in a large bowl.
2. Add the tomato juice, sherry vinegar, Worcestershire sauce, olive oil, salt, pepper, and fresh hot pepper to the chopped ingredients. Make sure to taste test as you go! (Once I added too much hot pepper, and at dinner, I could almost see steam rising from everyone's heads.) Some grams I know also add lemon juice!
3. Once you like what you have made, pop it into the refrigerator for a few hours. (You can save some time on this step by keeping all the ingredients cool beforehand.)
4. To serve, top with avocado slices. Or some toasted croutons. And maybe cilantro. ENJOY!

Congratulations! Felicitations! Felicidades! Gratulacje! Herzlichen Glückwunsch! Pongezi! Mazel tov!

There is no one right way to blend a family. Like soup, there are many recipes.

Many families celebrate multiple traditions. Others create brand-new celebrations.

The only mandatory ingredients for celebrating your family are patience, humor, and of course, lots and lots of love!

For Sylvie, Alice, and Emmett—S. A.
For Abby and Frank—A. L.

Helpful Resources

https://www.helpguide.org/articles/parenting-family/step-parenting-blended-families.htm
Resources and tips for newly blended families.

Miller, Susan Katz. *The Interfaith Family Journal*. Boston: Skinner House Books, 2019.
A resource with exercises, activities, and resources for interfaith families and couples. The author updates her blog regularly at https://onbeingboth.wordpress.com.

https://reformjudaism.org/site-search?search_api_fulltext=interfaith+families
Information and discussion on issues surrounding interfaith marriage in the Jewish community, including family questions, raising children, and more.

https://www.rewire.org/love/pieces-holiday-advice-interfaith-families/
Includes advice for new interfaith families from experienced interfaith families.

http://www.stepfamilies.info
Includes educational resources that address the unique issues faced by new stepfamilies.

Text copyright © 2022 by Sarah Aronson
Illustrations copyright © 2022 by Ariel Landy
All rights reserved, including the right of reproduction in whole or in part in any form. Charlesbridge and colophon are registered trademarks of Charlesbridge Publishing, Inc.

At the time of publication, all URLs printed in this book were accurate and active. Charlesbridge, the author, and the illustrator are not responsible for the content or accessibility of any website.

Published by Charlesbridge
9 Galen Street, Watertown, MA 02472
(617) 926-0329 · www.charlesbridge.com

Printed in China
(hc) 10 9 8 7 6 5 4 3 2 1

Illustrations were drawn and colored digitally
Display type set in Sugarstyle Millenial by Mats-Peter Forss
Text type set in Hunniwell by Aah Yes Fonts
Color separations and printing by 1010 Printing International Limited in Huizhou, Guangdong, China
Production supervision by Jennifer Most Delaney
Designed by Diane M. Earley

Library of Congress Cataloging-in-Publication Data
Names: Aronson, Sarah, author. | Landy, Ariel, illustrator.
Title: Brand-new bubbe / Sarah Aronson; illustrated by Ariel Landy.
Description: Watertown, MA: Charlesbridge, [2022] | Audience: Ages 4–7. | Audience: Grades K–1. | Summary: Jillian does not want another grandmother, after all she already has a Noni and a Gram, so when her mother marries Michael she is distinctly cool to her new bubbe—but her mother convinces her to give Bubbe a chance, and Jillian and all her grandmothers come together over a bowl of soup. Includes recipes for Matzo Ball Soup, Italian Wedding Soup, and Gazpacho.
Identifiers: LCCN 2020051071 (print) | LCCN 2020051072 (ebook) | ISBN 9781623542498 (hardcover) | ISBN 9781632897596 (ebook)
Subjects: LCSH: Grandmothers—Juvenile fiction. | Grandparent and child—Juvenile fiction. | Interfaith families—Juvenile fiction. | Multiculturalism—Juvenile fiction. | Soups—Juvenile fiction. | CYAC: Grandmothers—Fiction. | Family life—Fiction. | Soups—Fiction. | Jews—United States—Fiction.
Classification: LCC PZ7.A74295 Br 2022 (print) | LCC PZ7.A74295 (ebook) | DDC 813.6 [Fic]—dc23
LC record available at https://lccn.loc.gov/2020051071
LC ebook record available at https://lccn.loc.gov/2020051072

ONE WINTER'S NIGHT

ONE WINTER'S
~ NIGHT ~

Primrose Lockwood
Illustrations by Elaine Mills

HEINEMANN · LONDON

William Heinemann Ltd
Michelin House
81 Fulham Road, London SW3 6RB

LONDON   MELBOURNE   AUCKLAND

Text copyright © Primrose Lockwood 1991
Illustrations copyright © Elaine Mills 1991
0 434 94883 7
Produced by Mandarin Offset
Printed and bound in Hong Kong

For my nephew Joseph and his dog Timmy
and for Ben, Oliver, Lucy and Laura Sophie
at the farm on the hill.
P.L.

For Jenny
E.M.

Over a house the moon is shining.
Next to the house some trees are growing.
Inside the house a fire is burning.
Beside the fire a boy is sitting.
His name is Joseph.
What is he thinking?

From out of the house a man is going.
He's wearing a coat for the wind is blowing.
He's climbing the hill, but where is he going?
Where is he going now the moon is shining?
He's Joseph's father.
An owl is calling.

At the top of the hill there's a farmhouse standing.
It's silver and grey for the moon is shining.
Towards the farmhouse Joseph's father is striding.
From out of the shadows a fox is slinking.
It's frosty and cold.
The fox is watching.

In front of the farmhouse a gate is creaking.
Joseph's father goes through it. The gate he's latching.
The path to the house is long and winding.
In a barn somewhere a dog is barking.
Joseph's father goes up to the farmhouse door.
Why has he come? What is he seeking?

Inside the farmhouse children are listening.
Around a big table they're busily working.
One of them shouts, "Joseph's father is knocking!"
Along the passage their parents are hurrying.
They open the door.
Joseph's father is waiting.

With the moon to guide them the yard they're crossing.
From the window the children are watching.
They are leaning out and excitedly waving.
Across the yard the barn door is banging.
It's dark in the barn,
But a lamp is glowing.

Inside the barn the friends are talking.
Joseph's father is carefully looking.
When he comes out, a box he's carrying.
Inside the box something is moving.
He's taking the box to the house down the hill.
"Take care! Take care!" the children are calling.

At the house on the hill time is passing.
The hour is late. Joseph is sleeping.
His mother is busy. What is she making?
Down the hillside his father is coming.
Safe in his hands
Is the box he's carrying.

Early next morning Joseph is waking.
Into his room his parents are going.
They carry a box. "Come and see," they're calling.

Into the box Joseph is looking.
A puppy is there.
His tail is wagging.

"The puppy is yours," his parents are saying.
"Mine!" Joseph cries, hardly believing.
Carefully, carefully, the puppy he's holding.
Secretly, gently, its soft head he's stroking.
The puppy feels safe.
Joseph is smiling.

Out in the garden Joseph is running.
The puppy's there too, excitedly barking.
Laughing and leaping,
Together they're playing.

On the house on the hill,
The first flakes are falling.